Vivian French • Alison Bartlett

New Boots

Green Bananas

First published in Great Britain 2004
by Egmont Books Ltd
239 Kensington High Street, London W8 6SA
Text copyright © Vivian French 2004
Illustrations copyright © Alison Bartlett 2004
The author and illustrator have asserted their moral rights.
Paperback ISBN 1 4052 0873 2
10 9 8 7 6 5 4 3 2
A CIP catalogue record for this title is available from the British Library.
Printed in Singapore.

Bill Bird's
New Boots

When
Bill Bird
Went
Dancing

Hooray for
Bill Bird!

For Jack
V.F.
For Bathford Primary School
A.B.

Bill Bird's
New Boots

Bill Bird had new blue boots with laces.

He ran to show Molly Mouse and

Digger Rabbit.

'Look!' he said. 'Look at my new blue boots!'

'Wow!' said Molly. 'Cool boots!'

'Can you run fast in them?' asked

Digger. 'Let's run a race!'

'One two three GO!' said Molly.

CRASH! Bill fell over.

'Why did you fall over?' asked

Molly. 'Did you run too fast?'

'No,' said Bill. 'I fell over my laces.'

'Silly Bill!' said Digger. 'Why don't you tie them in a bow?'

'I don't know how,' said Bill sadly.

'Poor Bill,' said Molly. 'I'll tie them for you.'

'Now let's run a race!' said Digger.

Oh no! Digger fell over Molly, and

Molly fell over Bill.

CRASH!

When Bill Bird Went Dancing

Bill Bird wore his big blue boots
all the time.

He wore his boots to school.

He wore his boots to play football.

He wore his boots in his bath.

He even wore his boots in bed.

Bill Bird wore his boots to Molly

Mouse's dancing party.

Hello!

No one wanted to dance with him.

'Your boots are too big,' said Digger

Rabbit. 'You'll tread on our toes!'

'Bill,' said Molly, 'why do you wear your boots all the time?'

Bill went very red. 'I can't untie my

laces,' he said.

'Poor Bill,' said Molly. 'I'll untie them for you.'

'Hooray!' said Bill. 'Thank you!'

'Will you dance with me, Molly?'

asked Digger.

'Can I dance too?' asked Bill.

'YES!' said Digger and Molly.

Hooray for Bill Bird!

34

Bill Bird was walking to school with

Molly Mouse and Digger Rabbit.

'Hurry up, Bill!' said Molly.

'Hurry up, Bill!' said Digger.

'I can't,' said Bill. 'My boots are too big.'

Molly looked at Bill's boots.

'Where are your laces?' she asked.

Oh, Bill.

'In my school bag,' Bill said.

'Will you tie them for me?'

'No,' said Molly. 'I'll show YOU how to tie laces!'

Bill pulled the laces out of his bag.

Molly put them in his boots.

'Now,' Molly said, 'LEFT over RIGHT,

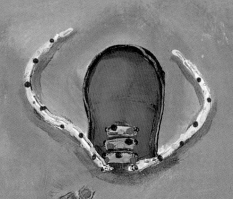

then UNDER and PULL!

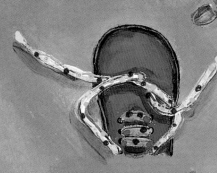

Loop up the RIGHT and loop up the LEFT,

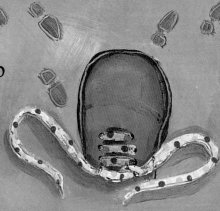

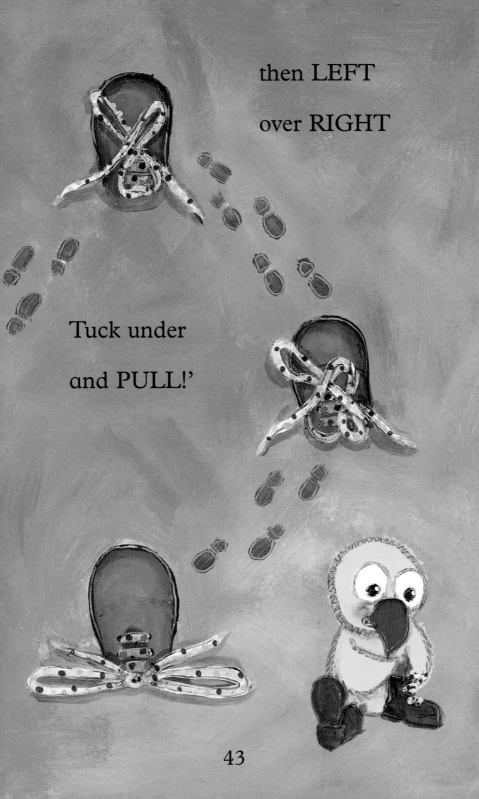

then LEFT

over RIGHT

Tuck under

and PULL!'

43

'WOW!' said Bill. 'Look, Molly!

Look, Digger! I tied my own laces!'

'Hooray for Bill!' said Molly.

'Hooray for Bill!' said Digger.

But Bill Bird said, 'Hooray for

Molly Mouse!'